The Wicked EDGE

NICOLE ELIZABETH

An imprint of Enslow Publishing
WEST 44 BOOKS™

Please visit our website, www.west44books.com.
For a free color catalog of all our high-quality books,
call toll free 1-800-542-2595 or fax 1-877-542-2596.

Cataloging-in-Publication Data

Names: Elizabeth, Nicole.
Title: The wicked edge / Nicole Elizabeth.
Description: New York : West 44, 2020. | Series: West 44 YA verse
Identifiers: ISBN 9781538382554 (pbk.) | ISBN 9781538382561 (library bound) | ISBN 9781538383285 (ebook)
Subjects: LCSH: Children's poetry, American. | Children's poetry, English. | English poetry.
Classification: LCC PS586.3 E459 2020 | DDC 811'.60809282--dc23

First Edition

Published in 2020 by
Enslow Publishing LLC
101 West 23rd Street, Suite #240
New York, NY 10011

This is a work of fiction. Names, characters, businesses, places, events, locales, and incidents are either the products of the author's imagination or used in a fictitious manner. Any resemblance to actual persons, living or dead, or actual events is purely coincidental.

Editor: Caitie McAneney
Designer: Seth Hughes

Photo Credits: Cover (background) © istockphoto.com/tamjkelly

Printed in the United States of America

CPSIA compliance information: Batch #CS18W44: For further information contact Enslow Publishing LLC, New York, New York at 1-800-542-2595.

Part One

MOM GOT THE JOB FIRST

Smoholla Indian School
on the Colville Reservation
in Omak needed teachers. And
Amanda Robbins had a degree.

She started teaching
fourth grade
in the K-12 tribal school.
Drove across the river

from Okanogan,
where we lived
and I went to school,
to Omak every day.

SOON SHE MET THE BOYFRIEND

which seems like
the wrong word
for the 46-year-old guy
whose trailer we live in now.

Damon Adams is a tutor
in Smoholla's reading program.
I guess it's hard to resist a man
who teaches kids to sound out words.

They fell in love across
sight words and stories
or whatever. *It was his charm
and commitment,* Mom says.

*It was my muscles and
my dreamy Native eyes.*
Damon flexes. And then he
started showing up to everything.

SOCCER GAMES AND BIRTHDAY PARTIES

When he stuck his pull-up bar
in Mom's bedroom doorway,

I knew he was going to
be around for a while.

It bothered me and my brother at first.
Someone around who wasn't Dad.

But we knew
that Damon was a good guy.

Mom was
suddenly happy.

He brought her joy.
She teased him

about being a meathead.
And he pretended to get sad

until she gave him a kiss.
They're always talking

about the stars.

MOM AND DAD NEVER FIT TOGETHER

Something I couldn't
understand for a long time.

The divorce happened fast.
As a kid, it seemed very sudden.

A twisted, wide tree,
splitting in a lightning strike.

After four years,
it's still hard to let go.

Dad moved to the East Coast.
As far as he could get, it seemed.

And we stayed in Washington.
We get to visit in the summers,

but I miss him. How can your dad
be your dad over a phone?

After, Charlie left too. He graduated
high school the year before last.

Mom decided she and I needed
something fresh.

Walls without her old memories
stuck in the trim and the paint.

SO WE MOVED TO DAMON'S TRAILER

Charlie left for Seattle.
Making his way at University of Washington
with a loud girlfriend and
all of his Dave Matthews CDs.

He was gone and,
like Dad, I knew
he wouldn't come back.
Why would he?

I am getting used to it.

The trailer is small,
but I have my own room.
For Mom, it's a half hour
closer to Smoholla.

It's also out of
Okanogan school lines.
So my mother decided
I would come to school with her.

YOU'RE DOING ME A FAVOR!

Mom reminded me
as I ate breakfast
on my first day—

a banana and a cheese stick.
I couldn't stomach
anything else.

It looks bad if the
teachers' kids don't go
where their parents work!

And about my friends:
You can still
see them on weekends!

And about not knowing anybody there:
This will be a challenge
you can rise to!

On second thought,
maybe just the banana.

I DIDN'T WANT TO LEAVE OKANOGAN

But if I was being honest, staying
wasn't turning out that great either.

High school had changed people.
Made it easier to get lost and

harder to be found. My friends
seemed to have it all figured out.

But I still felt unsure, like I was

tripping
along
behind
them.

I ROLLED MY EYES AT FOOTBALL GAMES

Couldn't make myself care about
chorus concerts and pep rallies.

I liked my hair how it was—
plain brown, curly, and frizzy in the heat.

It didn't matter to me
where the Freshman Fling was.

Or what they put
in the vending machines.

I just wanted what I knew.
What I thought I could count on.

Movies at Meghan's
on Saturdays.

Getting money from
Katie's dad for Dairy Queen.

Letting minnows in Omak Lake
eat the dead skin off our feet.

My friends didn't seem to
care about that stuff anymore.

MOM TOLD ME AGAIN IT WOULD BE FINE

You're a smart girl,
Helen, honey.
You'll figure it out.
You'll probably
change a little bit, too.

We got in the car and
my belly clenched.
I thought, maybe she's right.
I hoped maybe this time,
change could be good.

THE FIRST DAY

Almost nobody talked to me,
unless you count the laughs
when they found out my last name.

Helen White?
the teacher called out.
I raised my hand slowly.

Heads picked up from desks.
Fingers paused on hidden cell phones.
Two boys dropped the paper wad
they had been using as a basketball.

Everyone stared at me like they had been
waiting for this since I walked into class.

About 20 kids in the room,
in the *whole tenth grade*,
and 200 kids in the school.

I was the only white kid,
and my last name wouldn't
let anyone forget it.

MOM HAD WARNED ME ABOUT THIS

It's a tribal school
that teaches the cultural
language and customs
right beside English and Math.

It's a wonderful thing, she said.
And it's the only school like it
in the area. Your classmates
are all going to be Native.
You'll have to adjust to that.

I had Native classmates at Okanogan,
but not this many. I had never been in
the minority before. And I'd never ever
been the *only* white kid anywhere.

I was also the only White.
Mom had dropped Dad's name
after the divorce. Gone back to Robbins.

It quickly became a joke to my classmates.

THEY CALLED ME *WHITE*

every chance they could
for the next week.

In between classes,
Hey, it's White!

Picking teams in PE,
White!

Mocking me in the lunch line.
You want white milk, right? White?

I started to think of my own
name as an insult. I flinched

even when people
out of school used it.

At first the teachers seemed unsure
what to do. Then they banned

my last name altogether. I was
only allowed to be called Helen.

I THOUGHT I KNEW WHY

Thought I knew about
the Trail of Tears

and how white people
forced Native Americans

onto reservations and
tried to take away their culture.

I figured that was why
they hated me: history.

BUT AS THE TEASING CONTINUED

I realized
it wasn't about history.

It wasn't even really about
me being white.

It was about me being
an outsider, someone

they didn't know, and
who didn't know them.

I FELT IT

when I sat dumbly
in our Salish Language class. Or

when I thought the dance room was for ballet
and hip-hop instead of traditional dances.

In assemblies, I sat quietly
in the bleachers

while my classmates
drummed and sang.

I didn't want to screw up
words I didn't know. Thought

it would be wrong
to participate

because these traditions were
only for their people.

I DIDN'T UNDERSTAND

how I made myself look,
like I thought their culture
was below mine.

I didn't see that every time
I sat out from a round dance
or held my breath at a smudging,

when they burned
sage and sweetgrass
and spread the smoke

around us with
an eagle feather,
I set myself further apart.

Made it seem like
I had no interest
in their traditions.

SO THE BULLYING CONTINUED

Getting worse while I
thought I was being respectful.

I pulled myself
further and further away,

thinking I was hiding, but
really making myself a sitting duck.

I went everywhere alone.
Even ignored the kids who tried

to talk to me. I thought
everyone wanted to trick me.

I LIED TO MY MOTHER

I told her and Damon
that I was okay.

I didn't want them to know this
was another thing I just couldn't get

the hang of. They never really saw me
anyway. They were always in the Elementary wing.

I knew they were worried and
they probably knew I was lying.

But we all just kept hoping
this was going to work.

Part Two

AT FIRST, HIS EYES SCARED ME

Deep-set under
a sharp brow line,

they pinned
my feet down.

Stopped me dead—
frozen in the hallway.

As if they were
knives at my skin.

LIKE IF I MOVED

one

single

cell

my body might
burst and bleed

wild heartbeat
on the glossy tile.

HE SAT THERE IN THE DIM LIGHT

of the main office.
Arms crossed

over a cocky chest.
Shoulders leaned

too far back
in a tilted chair.

I thought this boy
was waiting

to say something rude.
Picking the perfect way

to point out that I
didn't belong

at this school.

BUT KING BIGELK

pulled the
flat brim of his hat

down lower over
those dark eyes

and smiled at me.
A shocking thing.

Lips just barely turned
like the sharp curve of a blade.

DO YOU NEED SOMETHING, HELEN?

I almost
couldn't remember

why I was there at all.
And then I felt

the attendance folder
in my hand.

I SNAPPED MY EYES

onto Front Desk Lady
and slid the folder

over the counter.
Attendance,

I spat out, trying
to keep my eyes from

flicking back to
the boy behind her.

GREAT, THANKS

She smiled back.
Then,

Hey, how are you
liking it here? Are
you getting to know
some people yet?
I know it can be
tough to move
to a new school.

ADULTS DID THIS TO ME SOMETIMES

They used that
extra-kind voice
to check on me.
Like I didn't know
they were doing it.

Like I couldn't tell
they were being nice
to make sure I didn't go
off myself in the bathroom
because I didn't have friends.

I get it. It's something
to show they care.
But getting asked
in front of other kids
was always embarrassing.

KING LAUGHED

A quick push of air
through his nose.
I looked back at him.

He wasn't scary anymore.
Just a kid in a room.
And his hat looked
dumb like that anyway.

But he had
a dare on his lips.

Go ahead,
I imagined him saying.

Lie to her about
how great it's been.
Tell her how happy you are.
Better yet, cry about how bad it is.

They both waited.

SOMETHING STIRRED IN ME

Something changed.

Old Helen would have
perked up at that question.

Lied straight through her teeth.
Said, *Yeah, things are great!*

It's what people expect
the teacher's kid to say.

And I guess that used to
be important to me.

BUT THERE WAS SOMETHING ABOUT

the way he was watching.

Like there was nothing I could do
that he wouldn't expect.

Like there was no way I could say anything
to show that I was interesting.

And he just wanted to see me
prove him right.

He thought he had me all figured out.

Everyone here did.

teacher's kid

white smart

honest

boring eager

happy scared **Target** alone snob

miserable helpful

good girl

shy new

predictable

IT DIDN'T MATTER WHAT WAS TRUE AND WHAT WASN'T

In the month since
I had arrived at Smoholla,
I had stopped existing as me.

Here
I was only
who everyone else
thought
I was.

Or
who I thought
everyone else
thought
I was.

So I guess
I had to
choose:

be who they saw

or

try to be someone else.

WHEN I FLIPPED HER OFF

I didn't even see
Front Desk Lady's face.
Helen!

Instead I stared
at the boy behind her.
Neither of us flinched.

Still,

when I walked away,
his soft, shallow laugh
followed me.

For the first time in weeks,
my mouth bloomed wide
into a smile.

I HAD HEARD OF KING

He was pretty
well known at school
for being
          wild.
I was never
very impressed
with stuff like that.

But seeing him
in the office
made me feel
          different.
I was hooked.
But I didn't know it yet.

KING WASN'T THE ONLY BIGELK AT SCHOOL

His sister, Kora,
went to Smoholla, too.

King was a senior and
Kora was a sophomore. Like me.

I learned very quickly
that they were at the top
of the food chain.

YOU COULD SEE IT

in the way they walked
down the hallway,

a bunch of kids
always around them.

Forever circling
like bodyguards

around a celebrity.
The other kids went by

without even looking
most of the time.

People didn't mess
with the BigElks.

And if they did,
they never did it again.

KORA WAS IN MY FIRST-PERIOD P.E. CLASS

For a few weeks,
I actually thought

she was being friendly.
She would watch me

stand alone while teams
were picked. Then she'd

point to signal
I should join hers.

She wouldn't use my name.
Wouldn't make people laugh at it.

KORA WOULD THROW ME THE BALL

from time to time,
even though

she knew
I'd miss the hoop.

She didn't talk to me, but
she didn't act like I didn't exist.

BUT THAT DAY I RAN INTO KING ...

I also ran into Kora.
She was coming

down the hallway.
A white late pass in her hand.

And she caught that smile
sliding over my face.

Kora's gaze flicked from me
to her brother and back.

I felt so good that
I even smiled at her.

THE NEXT MORNING

when I walked into P.E.
and started changing,

she came in.
Looked at me.

Then punched a locker.
Most of the girls flinched.

One with chin-length
hair and blue glasses

rolled her eyes
and walked out.

Kora's friends just laughed.
She started walking around,
eyes narrow.
Every few steps,

she would put her fist up
and slam the side of it

into another locker.

WHAT'RE YOU DOING?

One girl asked,
laughing.

I feel like hittin'
something. Kora's reply.

Her smile came
just like King's—

slight and wicked.
I left the locker room,

thinking someone must have
made her mad.

Out in the gym,
we grabbed basketballs

and shot around.
Waiting for the teachers

to come out
of their offices.

I stood off
to the left,

walking for
rebounds.

KORA CAME OUT

Her hands red
like berries.

She got a ball and crossed
to the far side of the gym.

She walked like an athlete.
Moved easily with a ball in her hand.

Her hair hung far down,
a long ponytail against her back.

It seemed to have her attitude,
waving and whipping

while she dodged her friends
and drove easily to the hoop.

Even across the entire gym,
we focused on her.

We watched her more
than our own shots.

THE TEACHERS HAD US PLAY

five-on-five basketball, boys and girls
at either end of the gym.

Ms. Neely stood off to the side to ref
while my team matched with the other.

Usually I just stood down by the hoop
since I was pretty tall.

I let other people come to me.
Today that person was Kora.

When another girl passed to me,
Kora came to life. I panicked,

looking for someone to
come and grab the ball from me,

but nobody did. All I could see
everywhere was Kora.

Then as if through a tunnel,
I started to hear Ms. Neely's voice:

SHOOT, HELEN!

You're tall enough.
Shoot over her head! Shoot it!

I swung the ball
over my head,

tried to zone in
on the hoop.

My right elbow came in
and I started to push up.

Felt the weight of the ball
starting to leave.

And then Kora jumped.

SHE DIDN'T JUST STUFF ME

It was like she
grabbed the ball with one hand

and threw it back in my face.
My eyes watered.

Ms. Neely's whistle
blew three sharp blasts

somewhere behind me.
When I could see again,

there were bright red marks
all over the floor and

all over my fingers.
Blood.

Come on, Kora!
Neely jogged toward us.

Holay, Kora!
someone said, surprised.

Girls laughed into
each other's shoulders.

It was an accident! Kora lied quickly.
Neely tried to help.

I JUST WANTED TO GET OUT OF THERE

I started moving
to the door,

the neck of my T-shirt
balled up against my face.

Then I heard Kora's
voice behind me.

Look, I'll make sure
she gets to the nurse, okay?

Her shoes squeaked when
she ran up behind me.

She put an arm over my shoulders
and led me out of the gym.

WHEN THE DOORS SHUT

the arm she had put around me
became tight and heavy.
She stopped us.

I knew something wasn't right.
I tried to keep walking, but
she gripped with both hands now.

She pushed me hard into a bathroom.
I fell onto the sinks. My hands smeared
red onto the green tile wall.

Whad are you doeeg!
I tried to yell, the question
stumbling out of my mouth.

She slid her fingers in the back of my hair
and shoved my head into the wall.
I heard a loose tile fall.

I slumped over and slid to the floor.
She kicked me hard, then she
grabbed under my chin.

I heard her voice close
behind my left ear:
Stay away from my brother.

MY EYES FLEW OPEN

and she was gone.

The bathroom door swung
shut with a whisper.

I slid my hand up the wall.

Planted my feet and tried to stand.
I spit out blood and tears and snot.

Then the door opened.

It was the girl from the locker room—
the one who had walked out.

Her mouth fell open when she saw me.

*Oh…woah…*she breathed.
She stepped into one of the stalls.

I heard her pulling toilet paper.

I stood over the sink,
trying not to look in the mirror.

Here. She came back to me.

I started cleaning my face. The paper
soaked quickly, thick with pink and red.

THE GIRL WATCHED QUIETLY

walking back and forth to
get me more toilet paper.

Her glasses were bright blue
and had horses on the sides.

My head pounded
where it had hit the wall.

And there was more blood
on my forehead.

Maybe we should get
some help...she said.

I didn't know what to do.
Could I trust her?

COULD I TRUST ANYBODY?

What would the nurse
and Ms. Neely tell my mom?

What would Kora and
this girl tell everybody else?

But I kept bleeding and
I was starting to get worried.

I nodded.
Before we left,

she checked
outside the door

to make sure no one
was out in the hallway.

When the coast was clear,
she took me upstairs.

INSTEAD OF GOING TO THE NURSE

she took me up to the tech office
of a teacher's aid named Z.

He took care of me
after a quick look.

Used a first-aid kit
that looked older than I was.

He wore a
Harley Davidson shirt,

jeans, and had a
short gray ponytail.

He watched me through small,
silver glasses with no frames.

Z NEVER ASKED QUESTIONS

Just gave a look
to the girl

as if to tell her
they would talk later.

When my nose
finally stopped bleeding, I spoke

for the first time
since leaving the bathroom.

Thank you, I mumbled.
I glanced at the girl, who sat

on a table against the wall.
What's your name, anyway?

I'm Taylor,
she said.

TAYLOR SHERMAN

walked me
back to class.

When she asked, I told her
what happened with Kora.

She and King
are really close,

and they don't like
when people

mess with their family.
Even a look can be enough.

I DIDN'T TELL TAYLOR EVERYTHING...

Not about giving
Front Desk Lady the finger.

Or how I did it to impress King
because I knew

he wouldn't expect it.
For some reason,

I wanted to keep
the truth of it

between me and King.
It felt special that way, and

I didn't want to admit
to someone else

how he had made me feel.
I didn't even know if it was real.

The truth also
didn't change the fact that

Kora beat me up
for no good reason.

WHAT ARE YOU GOING TO TELL PEOPLE?

I shrugged my shoulders. Looked
at the glare on the hallway floor.

I guess…that I fell
on the way up the stairs?

Yeah, that sounds good,
Taylor said.

Hey, I said. *Where were you, anyway?*
I remember you were in the locker room…?

She took a deep breath.
Oh yeah, well, I've been

at this school long enough
to know when something's

going to go down.

WHEN KORA STARTED HITTING THOSE LOCKERS

I went and told Neely
that I threw up

in the bathroom and
she sent me to the nurse.

I just went up
to sit in Z's room.

I WAS SURPRISED, EVEN IMPRESSED

He didn't make you
go back to class? I asked.

*I don't do it a lot...*she said.
He knows when I go there

I'm trying to stay out of trouble,
not get into it.

When I brought you upstairs,
he must've figured

that's what I had been
trying to stay away from.

I bobbed my head
in understanding.

But really, I felt
more scared than ever.

HOW OFTEN DID STUFF LIKE THIS HAPPEN?

Taylor stopped,
just when her fingers

had touched
the handle

of the gym door.
She looked at me.
So, after you've had
time to think,

Z's going to ask you
about it.

Getting hurt like this
has to be reported.

Taylor twisted her hands
together in front of her.

YOU CAN TELL HIM THE TRUTH

and Kora will
definitely get

in trouble. I mean,
she'll get a referral

on her permanent
record. But

I don't know
what that would

do for you.
She tilted her head

to the side.
Honestly, it might

just make your life worse.
She'll know you talked.

I'D THOUGHT ABOUT THAT ALREADY

Figured the way to
stand up to someone here

wasn't going to be
through getting them

lunch detention or a visit
with the principal.

Maybe for now
I should just

stay away from her,
I said. Taylor nodded.

And King,
she added.

AFTER KORA BEAT ME UP

I did stay away
from her.

I moved to another row
in the locker room with Taylor.

If I saw Kora in class
or in the hallways,

I didn't look at her.
Finally having a friend

made this much
easier to deal with.

I STUCK WITH TAYLOR

She was funny. A quiet girl
full of opinions.

Every time a teacher
spoke in class,

Taylor would talk
under her breath to me,

or even just to herself,
about the subject.

With her face bent low
to her paper, writing notes.

I thought it was amazing
that she could listen, write,

and talk all at the same time.
I wondered how I had never

heard her doing this before,
never really noticed her.

Some people come into your life
right when you need them.

AND I NEEDED TAYLOR

She didn't seem
to be very popular.

But she got along
with people easily.

Could treat anybody
like a friend.

She blended with
different groups—

the nerdy kids, edgy kids,
the kids who acted like

they weren't in any group,
when really that made them a group.

I guessed it was because
she had grown up here.

People saw me with her
and I felt like I had passed a test.

She made it almost okay
for me to be here. She was my *in*.

HOW LONG HAVE YOU BEEN AT SMOHOLLA?

I asked her this
at lunch

a couple weeks after
she found me in the bathroom.

Since kindergarten.
I'm a lifer.

What's a lifer?

It was a Wednesday—
salad day.

She poked at lettuce
with her white plastic fork.

It means I'll be here
from kindergarten to senior year.

Me and my
brother both will.

YOU HAVE A BROTHER?

I took a sip of
my chocolate milk.

She sat up straight on
the bench.

Squeezed her eyebrows
and looked at me hard.

Yep.

I wasn't sure why
her tone had changed.

Is he older or younger?
Have I met him?

I looked around the cafeteria
like he might be there.

He's older, she said.
A senior. His name's Harry.

I nodded.
She kept going.

HE'S A SPED KID

What's a sped kid?

Like Special Ed, she said. *He's slow.*

I didn't know what to say.
Does he have, like, autism?

No, she said.
She looked like
she didn't know
if she wanted to tell me.
But she kept talking.

My mom…she used to do a lot of
drinking and drugs. And she did it
when she was pregnant with Harry.
So he was born…slow.

Then my mom went to rehab.
My grandma took care of Harry.
When I was born,
she took care of me, too.

TAYLOR TOOK A BREATH

But then my Mom got clean.
Now she takes care of us.
And she's a good mom.
And Harry's a good brother.

She looked at me.

Some people can be
really mean to him.

I bet, I said, knowing
what it was like to get bullied.

She kept looking at me,
her face like a warning.

I was eager to change
the subject.

DO YOU GUYS KNOW EVERYBODY HERE?

I asked. Taylor ripped open
a bag of croutons
and dumped it over
her little pile of salad.

Mmmm…A lot of people
move around, bounce
to different schools.
But yeah, I know most of them.

Different tribal schools?
I asked.

She looked sideways.
Yeah, sometimes.
But just because we're Native
doesn't mean we only go to Native schools.
I have cousins who go to your old school.

Right, I said, feeling
my face heat up.

The sense of not belonging
pulsed through me again.

HAS YOUR MOM STOPPED FREAKING OUT?

Taylor asked.

I thought back to
when I had made it

to Mom's classroom to go home
on the day Kora hit me.

The look on her face
when she saw

my bruises and bandages.
How she dropped

what was in her hands
and came right over to me.

HELEN, HONEY...

I had almost cried then.
I wasn't expecting it.

A wave of her care
hit me full in the chest

and the tears pooled
in my eyes.

I blinked them away
while she hugged me to her.

WHAT HAPPENED?

she had asked,
letting me go

and looking closer
at my head.

*I got hit with a basketball
and got a bloody nose.*

*Then I fell on the stairs
on the way to the nurse.*

Since I knew the real story,
the lie sounded so fake.

Just like it had when I told
Z that was what happened.

I DIDN'T THINK MY MOM WOULD BELIEVE IT

But as she pulled
back my hair

to see the cut
on my forehead,

I realized that she
trusted me. Because

she had no reason
to think I would lie.

OLD HELEN WOULDN'T HAVE LIED

Old Helen would have
turned Kora in,

would have done it
without thinking twice.

Because that was
the "right" thing to do.

People who hit other people
should get in trouble.

And Mom knew
I believed that.

But for this new,
different Helen,

things weren't so black and white,
so easy to understand.

I was mad about
what happened to me.

I was mad
Kora got away with it.

SO WHAT COULD I DO ABOUT IT?

I wasn't going to
tell my Mom

like a little girl.
Not anymore.

I know you don't want me
to treat you like a little kid,

Mom had said. I almost
thought I had spoken out loud.

But I wish you had come to
tell me you were hurt.

She kissed me on the forehead.
I smiled to say sorry.

Let's go home.

WHEN WE GOT TO THE TRAILER

Mom had fussed over me more
while filling Damon in

on what happened.
He looked at me evenly.

Hit with a basketball
and tripped on the stairs, huh?

Pretty clumsy
for a soccer player.

I stared back. Said,

Yeah. Bad day.

He gave a small nod and
continued to drink his coffee

from the couch.
He could sense

I was lying, but he didn't
push it any further.

I went into my room
and shut the door.

MOM TRIED TO CHECK ON ME A DOZEN TIMES

through the rest
of that night.

Kept knocking or
walking past when

she thought I couldn't
see her shadow below the door.

That's what Taylor
was asking about at lunch.

She's getting over it,
I said to Taylor.
Slowly.

Taylor laughed and then
stopped suddenly.

She looked up behind me.
I turned around.

Standing there
was King BigElk.

NONE OF US SAID ANYTHING

King sat down next to me.
His black Nike hoodie was

bunched around his neck.
His hat shaded his face

from the cafeteria lights.
He always seemed to be in the dark.

He held one fist with another.
He looked down at them as he

clenched and released his knuckles.
I glanced over at Taylor,

who looked annoyed.
Finally he spoke, meeting my gaze.

ABOUT WHAT HAPPENED IN THE GYM...

he started.
I didn't say anything.

Kora's tough.
Sometimes people get hurt.

Taylor snorted from across the table,
then took a bite of salad.

I searched rapidly through my brain
for something to help me know

what was going on here.
What did he want?

Did he know Kora told me
to stay away from him?

I just thought maybe...you'd
let me make it up to you.
Like...say sorry.

STILL I STARED AND SAID NOTHING

Where have you been for two weeks…
I heard Taylor say to her tray.

I noticed people
starting to whisper

behind his shoulder,
looking at us

and tilting their heads.
A group of boys laughed.

They clearly thought
this was a joke.

I looked at Taylor and she had
one eyebrow up and one down.

She'd been chewing the same mouthful
of salad for way too long now.

No one trusted this. I shouldn't either.
New confidence rose in me.

I took a breath
and answered him.

I DON'T CARE ABOUT YOUR "SORRY"

and I don't care
about your sister.
How about you just
stay away from me?

Now I waited for him,
not looking away. I stared
straight into the
shadow of his face.

He just smiled—
a comma in his cheek—
and more anger
flooded my brain.

We'll see, he said. Then
he pushed off the table
and walked away.
I squinted my eyes.

TAYLOR HAD A SMIRK ON HER FACE

Nice, she said.
I almost believed you.

What does that mean?
But I knew my neck
was getting red again.

Oh, King, she said
in a fake voice,
stay away from me.

She waved her fork around
in the air while she pretended to

flip her hair. Ranch dressing
flew off the end of it.

I bit down hard on my lip
to keep from laughing.

WHATEVER

I said.
I think he's gross.

Not even! she shot back.
You're into him.

I am not! I said loudly.

She laughed and fixed her glasses.
Ayez. He is gross though.

We stood up to scrape our trays into the trash.

WHAT'S THAT?

The word sounded like more than one "a."

"Ayez" means, like, "just kidding" or "jokes."

Did you make that up? I asked.

No. It's just a thing we say, she said.

Huh. I tested it out. *Ayez.*

She looked at me with
both eyebrows up.

What?

She walked away laughing.

PEOPLE HAD HEARD ABOUT KING AND ME

Even in the next class,
I got looks from kids

that I knew were about him.
Kora sat at the edge of her seat

and focused on the board.
She never looked at me.

Her foot bounced
nonstop under her desk.

WHISPERS FOLLOWED ME

in the hallways. Taylor

made faces, saying things
like, *Jeez, all you did was*

sit there while he talked at you…
I asked myself if that was really

all that happened.
I wondered,

secretly hoped,
would it happen again?

AT THE END OF THE NEXT DAY

I sat on the sidewalk
in the parking lot waiting

for my mom. I watched
students get on the buses.

King and Kora
stood alone to the side.

They were talking, King relaxed
with his hands in the pockets

of his joggers, Kora holding the straps
of her backpack. Her eyes squinting

against the sun. She looked at him.
He kept looking away.

AFTER A WHILE

one of the buses honked
and Kora turned to yell

something at the driver.
He must have been waiting for her.

She and King gave each other
a one-armed hug. Then she

ran up the steps of the bus.
King crossed the circle

to the parking lot.
He was coming right toward me.

I TRIED THE CAR DOOR HANDLE

even though I knew
it was locked. Then I turned away

from King and took out my phone,
pretending to text someone.

I thought about answering a fake call
when he came up next to me.

I kept my eyes locked on my phone.
You talking to someone about me?

His voice was deep and smooth.
It annoyed me. I didn't look up.

YOU ALWAYS THINK EVERYONE IS TALKING ABOUT YOU?

I asked.

He laughed in one small sound.

You remind me of my sister, he said.

Maybe I should punch you then, I said.

He sucked in air through his teeth.

Maybe you should…

When I finally looked up,
his face was sad for just a moment.
Then it smoothed into an easy grin.

SO WHEN ARE WE GONNA HANG OUT?

he asked, jiggling his keys
in front of my face.

We're not, I said.

I started to walk
back toward the school.

I knew he was watching me.
Why was he trying so hard?

I'm going to get you
to be nice to me!

he called out just before
I reached the doors.

He was too far away
to hear me laugh.

WHEN MOM AND I DROVE HOME

I noticed a
stiffness between us.

She didn't say much,
just polite stuff

about what was
on the radio.

Then after a
stretch of quiet,
she talked.

Helen, I have to ask you about
something I heard today.
Something about you.

RIGHT AWAY

I thought of
Kora's attack and

looked out the window
at the sage bushes and rocky hills.

My big secret.

I felt guilty for not telling her,
and I was almost glad that

she had finally heard and
would be able to help me.

Okay, I mumbled.

BUT IT WASN'T KORA SHE WANTED TO TALK ABOUT

It wasn't me getting hurt,
or me being bullied at all.

Someone told me today
that you flipped off a staff member
a couple weeks ago.

I felt something
roll through me.

It mixed with my blood,
bubbled and steamed

in my throat.
Oh…

HALF OF ME WANTED TO CRY

It was on the
tip of my tongue

to tell her about Kora.
I wanted her to help me,

tell me what to do.
But when Mom asked

why I would do that,
the other half of me grew angry.

Ticked off in a way that I had
never been at my mom before.

ANGRY

that she hadn't found out
the real reason why I got hurt.

that she hadn't been there
to protect me.

that she couldn't see
how much I needed her.

that all she seemed to care about was how I
made her look bad.

IN A WEIRD WAY, IT FELT GOOD

to hold these
things against her.

Make them her fault.
She was the reason I was hurting,

why I was even at Smoholla.
She made me come here.

She said it would be okay.

I COULD TALK ABOUT

the fight we had.
All the ugly words
we said.

How more lies spilled
out of my mouth—easier now—
fueled by pain and anger.

How even Taylor came up
in the yelling, someone
for my Mom to blame.

But maybe,
of all the words in a fight,
only the worst ones really matter.

NO

wonder

Dad

didn't

love

you.

All

you

care

about

is

yourself.

Mom's face fell,
broken like glass.

I SAT ON MY BED UNTIL DARK

breathing heavily and
squeezing my pillow.

Because Mom only
thought she knew

everything. But
she had no idea

how big the
real picture was.

She was living a
happy new life

with her new job
and new boyfriend.

ALL SHE KNEW ABOUT ME

was that
I was still part of

that old life.
The one she hated

so much. The one
I missed so much

before everything
got ruined.

My face was hot.
The tips of my fingers,

white under my nails,
pressed into the pillow.

Then I heard
tapping on my window.

I ALMOST CALLED OUT FOR MOM

but I stopped myself.
I sat perfectly still. Waiting

to see if I would hear it again.
I half believed that I had made it up

in my own head. But then it came again.
Barely a sound, it was so quiet.

I stood up silently. Walked lightly
across my room so I wouldn't make

any noise. Then I grabbed the corner
of my curtain and pulled it back.

KING STOOD OUTSIDE THE TRAILER

lit up by the
flashlight on his phone.

He wore all black
and had his hood up.

He looked like a spy
who was about to

climb onto the roof
and defuse a bomb.

But instead he waved
his hand to the side,

telling me to slide
the window open.

I LOOKED BACK AT MY DOOR

No shadow underneath.
I could hear Damon

watching ESPN
in the living room.

I went to the white noise
machine next to my bed and

flipped the switch
on. Just in case.

Then I
opened the window.

KING'S TEETH

seemed to sparkle
in the dark
when he said my name.

Hey, Helen. What's up?
I stared down at him.

What do you mean, "What's up?"
What are you doing here?

He looked like this was normal.
Like he did this all the time.
Like we did this all the time.

I thought you might
want to hang out, he said.

Hang out? It's 9:30! I said.
How do you know where I live?

HE SHRUGGED

Asked some people.
I think your mom's
boyfriend is my cousin
or uncle or something.

I looked down at him and
didn't know what to say.

I can't!

I shook my head back and forth.
That was the right answer.
I wasn't one of those girls in movies
who climbed out her window
at night to be with a boy.

Can't?

He laughed.

Do you want to?

DID I WANT TO?

Was it
really that easy?

I thought about
my mom and Kora

and the kids at school
who still whispered things

when Taylor wasn't with me.
I thought about how

I kept trying
to do what was right,

and none of it made anything better.
None of it made me happy.

WHEN WAS THE LAST TIME

I had felt really
good about something?

A face popped into my head.
The face of a boy with a flat brim

pulled low, who smiled like he had
a trick under his tongue. A boy

who looked at me like he could
see under my skin. A boy who

kept finding me over and over again,
asking me to come with him.

And all I had to do
was want to.

I GRABBED THE TENNIS SHOES

next to my door and
shoved my feet into them quickly.

Then I dragged my desk chair
over to the window

and climbed into it, feet dangling
against the side of the trailer.

It's higher than I thought, I said,
trying not to sound scared.

Yeah, he said.
You're gonna have to jump. Here.

He reached up
so I could grab his hand.

I held onto it tightly and
let myself fall over the edge.

Part Three

FOR A LONG TIME WE JUST DROVE AROUND

talking in his truck—a lifted, black
Ford Lariat. It had heated front seats

and a custom stereo he had put in.
A braid of sweetgrass lay across

the dashboard. An eagle feather
hung from the rearview mirror.

I took my shoes off and
pulled my legs up

in the passenger seat.
I leaned over with my

back against the cold window.
Winter was coming soon.

I grew more comfortable
as the drive went on.

The darkness settled nicely into
the empty space of the roomy cab.

I LEARNED ABOUT HIS LIFE

How Kora lives with their
grandpa in first HUD.

The HUDs were cheaper housing
for families with lower income.

King lived there too before moving
in with friends, a group of boys

all out of high school already.
His "crew," he called them.

Why'd you move out? I asked.

He shrugged.
Things happen.

Parents? I asked.

Mom's in rehab again.
Never met my dad.

HOW DO YOU HAVE SUCH A NICE TRUCK?

I asked him, thinking back to
Charlie's friends' busted cars

when he was in high school.
Did someone buy this for you?

He snorted, his face tinted
green from the radio lights.

No. I got it with my eighteen money.

What's eighteen money?

He pulled off onto another
unmarked mountain road.

I had no idea where we were,
which struck me as stupid.

I had lived next to this town
my whole life, but I'd never seen

what King was showing me.

WHEN YOU'RE ENROLLED IN OUR TRIBE

you get money when
you turn eighteen.

For what?

He shrugged his shoulders.

For whatever you want.
Not every tribe does it.

Enough money to buy a truck?
I asked.

Oh yeah. Well. Depends on
when you enrolled. And I think

some other stuff. But I've been
enrolled as a tribal member

since I was a baby, so I got
a good chunk of money

a few months ago.

I LEANED TOWARD HIM

my elbows on the armrest.

You didn't want to save it? Like, for college?

He chewed a piece of gum.

That's Kora's big plan. Not mine, he said.

How come? I asked.

He shrugged his shoulders again.

Just ain't.

So what's your big plan? I asked.

And there was the smile.

I only got plans for tonight.

AFTER A WHILE

we popped onto the highway,
then took a right onto
a long, winding road.

The HUDs came into view.
He pulled into second HUD,
number two out of three.

We drove to a stretch of cracked,
weedy blacktop. He turned around
and backed the tailgate up to its edge.
He parked and turned the truck off.

I HOPPED OUT AFTER HIM

looking up
at the stars. They
seemed so close.

King dug through the back seat,
then pulled out a basketball.
I groaned.

What? He laughed, bouncing it
through his legs as he walked
toward me.

I don't have very good luck
with this sport, remember?
I pointed to my nose.

The coloring was normal now,
but it was still tender.
I wiggled it at him.

We better make some new luck, then.
He passed me the ball
before I could say no.

WE PLAYED

stupid kid games. HORSE
and Around the World.

He tried not to laugh
every time I air-balled.

I gagged when he
made a half-court shot.

He surprised me, ran up
all pretend-mad.

I surprised him,
stood my ground.

HE CLOSED IN

got right in my face,

going for the classic
start-something pose.

I put one eyebrow up
and stuck out my chin.

When are you going to learn?
You don't scare me, King BigElk.

When he laughed, he was so close,
I could feel his breath on my lips.

I took one step backward
but he caught my waist,

pulling me back to him.
Holding me with both hands.

Are you sure?
he whispered.

When he kissed me,
I decided I wasn't

sure of anything.

I WANTED MORE

Mom and I
weren't really talking.

And that gave me
a good reason

to go to my room
straight after dinner every night.

After about an hour,
I would text King

that it was all clear.
Then I would wait

for his flashlight to
show under the flap of

curtain that I started to
keep pulled back.

MAYBE MY MOM STARTED TO CATCH ON

Maybe she and Damon
could hear me leaving.

Maybe she came to my room
one night when I was gone.

Maybe once I
imagined my Mom,

standing in the dark window
when we drove away.

But maybe I didn't.
No one said anything to me.

And even if they had,
I wasn't going to stop.

I IGNORED MY DAD'S PHONE CALLS

I wondered if Mom had said anything
to him. Then I stopped caring.

Finally something was going
how I wanted it to,

and I wasn't giving that up,
no matter what.

Besides, if my Dad didn't care
when he left me here,

why should he start now?
And why should I?

KING'S PLACE

His friends were
always partying.

It showed me a
whole new kind of life.

They would work
during the day,

some doing odd jobs,
security at the casino,

construction…Then
they would come home

just to stay up all night.
Mostly to drink beer

and smoke, showing
any number of girls

the way to their bedrooms.

THE NEXT MORNING

they would get up
and do it all over again.

When I sat on the couch
next to King,

I was stunned by
their ability to rise

every morning
without sleeping more

than four hours a night.

SOON I WAS JOINING IN

I threw away Old Helen
for good, fitting into
this new person's life.

New Helen had gotten
what Old Helen hadn't.

Acceptance.

I loved her for the way she
finally made me feel in control.
I loved her for being brave,

for being exciting,
and for getting

King.

BEER IS BEST

when cold,
I found.

And pot brownies
taste a lot better

than a joint does.
Tequila hits

like lighter fluid
and vodka is only good

when you have
something to go with it.

Whiskey burns
all the way down

and hard cider is the sweetest.
But nothing, nothing was as good

as Kora's face when
she saw me with King.

IT WAS A THURSDAY NIGHT

There was snow on the ground now,
Christmas break.

Kora came pounding
on the door.

There were cans and cups
all over the room.

And a group of us were
hanging out, smoking, watching

Monsters, Inc. and laughing.
I had just been explaining

a subplot I found
and there she was.

Looking down
at me on the floor

with my legs stretched
in front of me. King's head

lay in my lap.
He didn't sit up

when his sister walked in,
and I was pinned under him.

HEY, KID

King said. He took a long hit,
then passed to his friend Chase.

Don't call me that,
she snapped back at him.

But she was staring at me.
Her face twisted into a scowl,

and she shook her head.
I looked back at her

and felt strong.
Maybe this had been

the best way to get back at her
all along. Now that King and I

were together,
she wouldn't touch me.

SHE FOCUSED BACK ON KING

Grandpa needs
to talk to you.

Sounds good,
he said lazily,

drawing out the words,
not looking at her.

King! she yelled,
and the group laughed.

It was so different,
I thought,

to see her in a
place with no power.

She looked like a little kid,
begging for attention.

C'MON, KORA

Chase said from the couch.
Have a beer. You can sit next to me.

Kora swore at him,
telling him exactly

what she thought of that idea.
King finally sat up.

Shut up, Chase, he said.
His voice was serious and final.

Chase's eyes stayed on Kora.
He took a long sip of his beer.

The room grew quiet and
the air seemed to shiver.

King locked eyes with Kora.
I almost thought they were

talking with their minds.

KING SPOKE FIRST

Tell him I don't care. I'm not going.

He wants to talk to you about it, Kora repeated.

Well I don't want to talk to him, Kora!
Jeez...since when does she care about us?

She's our mom, Kora said.

She's not my mom! And I don't know
when she was yours neither!

King—

—Grandma was more of a mom
than she was! Grandma was my mom.

King grabbed the TV remote
and turned the volume up loud.

Kora's eyes, for one second,
looked defeated.

She turned and walked
back out the door.

Part Four

SOMETHING CHANGED AFTER THAT NIGHT

King had never been
totally calm. He was

always looking for
the next thing to do,

could never sit still. Now
he was jumpier

than I had ever seen.
He spent hours

in the weight room at school.
His teachers didn't

seem to mind because
it kept him from disrupting class.

Sometimes I saw the counselor
going in and out of there,

a shiny black binder in his hand.

WHEN KING PICKED ME UP

at night he blasted electric
powwow music

or heavy rap.
No longer worried

about being quiet.
There were no more

stories or questions.
We barely talked at all.

He also drank more often. He got
suspended for bringing weed

to school in his backpack.
It was like he wanted to get caught.

I HADN'T REALLY TALKED TO TAYLOR IN WEEKS

King had been skipping
his sixth-period class

to come to my lunch
almost every day.

We'd sit together
at our own table

before he'd get
kicked out.

Then I'd spend the last
five minutes with Taylor.

WHEN KING STOPPED SHOWING UP AT LUNCH

I turned to Taylor again.
She was all I really had left.

He wants to hang out
every night now, I said.

Taylor shifted in her seat,
ate a French fry.

Her eyes squinted.
You're not sleeping with him,
are you?

No! I said quickly.
He just…likes to be close to me.

Taylor made a face. I said,
I just mean he's always
sitting really close

or touching my leg or my arm.
Always asking me to kiss him.

Possessive, much?
asked Taylor.

THE TRUTH WAS

I hadn't really
thought of it like that.

I was just happy to be wanted.
But I found I couldn't

admit that to Taylor.
No…he likes me, I said,

and the air changed.
She knew I was annoyed.

He trusts me, I added.
He leans on me.

Taylor looked at me quietly,
ate another fry.

*He told you that his grandma died
just before school started, right?*

THE ANSWER WAS NO

Yeah, I lied.
Taylor adjusted her glasses.

It was really sad, she said.
She was a cool woman,

helped a lot of people.
King was a wreck.

Didn't go to the funeral.
He was out partying all the time.

A lot like he is now,
from what I've heard.

Then Kora would go out and find him,
bring him back home.

I SAT STIFFLY IN MY SEAT

prickling because she
knew this and I didn't.

We talked about that, I said. Another lie.
How do you know about it?

She shrugged.
Small town.

Just like that, I was
an outsider again.

We ate in silence for a while.
I finished my tray and got up to go.

HELEN, WAIT

I paused
next to the table,

wanting to leave. But
Taylor's face was serious.

You need to be careful, she said.
I held her stare.

What do you mean?
She stood up to talk in a low voice.

I've heard things about King.
About when he gets like this.

What things? I asked.

SCARY THINGS

Taylor said. I looked
at her and felt angry again.

A feeling that I seemed
to have all the time now.

You don't know him, I said.

Do you? she asked.

NOW I SURROUNDED MYSELF WITH KING

We texted all the time,
mostly about nothing.

I talked to his friends.
The same kids who made my life awful

were now the ones I let
copy my homework.

If I even did homework at all.
I wrote him letters in class,

which I left in his locker
or stuffed in his backpack.

Before King,
I was just the white girl at school.

With King, I was the white girl
who hung out with King BigElk.

KING HAD TURNED ME INTO SOMEONE

Someone
who belonged.

I just couldn't
go back

to the way
things were before,

when people
hated me and

I was alone.
Now maybe they

still hated me, but
at least I had somebody.

I wasn't alone,
wasn't afraid,

and it was all
because of King.

I IGNORED TAYLOR

But her warning
stuck in my brain.

Sometimes I thought
about slowing down,

telling King I needed
a break. But the thought

of losing him, of seeing
him with a new girl who

could keep up with him,
was too much.

I needed him, and I
told myself he needed me.

WE SPENT ALL OF OUR FREE TIME TOGETHER

I snuck out
almost every night.

Didn't bother
to cover my tracks

when the snow came and went.
I drank more, smoked more.

It was the only way
I knew how to

hang out with him.
I feared he was getting

bored with me,
so I tried to surprise him.

I started cutting my classes
to show up in his study halls.

Or we'd plan to get in trouble
at the same time so

we'd be sent to the ISS room
together and could annoy the teacher.

I WON'T PRETEND IT WASN'T EXCITING

Every day I got to
be someone who was liked.

Someone who was cool
because she wasn't afraid.

At least,
she didn't think
she was afraid.

BEFORE THIS YEAR

I never understood
how much

my life was made of
my own choices.

Wanting to impress King
showed me that

I didn't *have* to
go to my next class.

I didn't *have* to
get good grades.

I didn't *have* to
be happy and smiling.

I didn't have to be anything.

I didn't even have to be kind.

Part Five

THE DAY IT HAPPENED

I had walked out
of my English class.

I didn't care about
what we were learning.

So I just picked up my stuff
and walked out the door.

A year ago, I never would have
thought that was even possible.

THE HALLWAY WAS QUIET AT FIRST

I could hear
the hum of the lights

and the muffled voices
of teachers talking behind

closed classroom doors.
I strolled in the direction

of my locker.
Then I saw him.

HE WAS VERY TALL AND VERY SKINNY

He wore baggy, light-wash
jeans that were ripped

at the bottom
where his ankles

poked out over chunky
black basketball shoes.

He had a puffy green coat on
and his hair was short, jet black.

It looked wet.

I KNEW AS SOON AS I SAW HIS FACE

that this was Taylor's brother, Harry.
He wore glasses,

like Taylor, and
he had the same

sharp, high cheekbones.
Right then they were

flushed red and
I realized he was sweating.

HARRY'S BACKPACK STRAPS

had been pulled
up all the way

so that they hugged
his shoulders tightly.

The rest of the straps
hung down to his sides,

and one was stuck
in his locker.

It must have happened
when he was walking away.

He was turned
so that he couldn't

get around to
open the locker again

and the shoulder straps
were too tight.

He couldn't figure out
how to get his arms out.

HE WAS TRYING TO TUG HIMSELF FREE

but he was stuck.
He panted quietly,

his bottom lip
hanging down.

I looked around
and wondered

where the teachers were
who helped him.

Then I thought, he's been
going here since kindergarten.

He's probably gone to his locker alone
a hundred times by now.

This is
just a freak accident.

I WALKED OVER

Hey...Harry, right?

He stared at me and
nodded his head.

Some spit fell in a
thread from his mouth.

He was definitely
starting to overheat

from pulling so hard.
Drops of sweat were

sliding down his neck
behind his ears.

His orange T-shirt was
dark around the neckline.

WE'VE GOTTA GET YOU OUT OF THAT COAT

I said. I reached out
to try to push

the shoulder strap down,
but Harry didn't like that.

When I made contact,
he let out a loud sound.

It wasn't a word, but
I knew he was yelling at me

to stop touching his coat.
Okay, I said, and backed off,

but he started to struggle harder.
I put my hands up in front of me

and tried to get him to calm down.
It's okay, I said loudly.

I JUST WANT TO GET YOU OUT

I said. His eyes
were growing wider

and his breathing
was getting harder.

He started to twist
his whole body fast

to the left and right.
On one turn I thought

he was going to
smack his head

into the locker.
Without thinking,

I reached out and grabbed
his head in my hands.

THERE SEEMED TO BE A PAUSE

while we both felt
what was happening.

But my brain didn't
tell my hands

to let go of Harry's head
as fast as I needed it to.

Before my fingers were
an inch away, he

swung his hand up
and slapped my face.

THEY SAY THAT HINDSIGHT IS 20/20

That means it's easier to see
how you could have acted,

should have acted,
after you've already

done something
and you're looking

back on it. It's easy to
point to the past and say,

Here's where I went wrong.
But in the moment,

sometimes you have
no idea what you're doing,

or why.
Sometimes you're not

thinking at all.
Or maybe that's just

what we tell ourselves
to feel better about

what we've done.

WHAT WAS I THINKING

when I looked back at Harry
and yelled at him?

Was I using my brain
when I called him a *retard*?

What choice was I making
when I slipped my phone

out of my back pocket?
Or when I took a picture

of him, flapping his arms
in fear before Z finally heard

what was going on
and rushed in to help?

treated Harry that way.

I SHOULD NOT HAVE

taken that picture.

sent it to King and his friends with the words, *At least your life isn't this rough.*

gone for a teacher right away.

I SHOULD HAVE

known Harry didn't really mean to hit me.

found Taylor and told her what happened.

SEE?

None of that
makes it any better.

IT DIDN'T TAKE LONG FOR THE PICTURE TO GET AROUND

The principal
called for me on the
PA system that day.

In the office,
I found my mother
already sitting there.

My stomach
twisted in shame.
We had stopped

talking much by then,
unless she had to yell at
or ground me again.

Now
she didn't even
look at me.

Amanda Robbins
had never
been speechless.

I WOULD BE SUSPENDED

until Harry's mother decided
what course of action
she wanted to take.

It was noted that
legal steps might be
taken against me.

And I was to go
to Alternative School
until further notice.

My mother sat and fumed
in the chair next to me.
My own throat swelled.

She didn't bother
sticking up for me.
I didn't bother

to defend myself,
or try to lie again.

I HAD CROSSED A LINE

I knew that as soon
as I had done it.

But it was done,
already in the past.

On the way home,
I couldn't even
look at my mother.

I could feel the hurt,
could feel the disgust.

I tried to break the silence,
to start making this right
somehow, as if I could.

Mom…I'm sorry—
She put her hand up,

stopped me before
I could say anything.

THE LOOK ON HER FACE

was horrible. She
was so ashamed of me.

Don't, she said.
Don't you even say
sorry to me.

What you did
to that boy...

I just sat there.
The tears
came quickly now.

Where is my daughter?
Her voice broke.

Where are you, Helen?

WHERE WAS I?

I felt like I had been
standing on this ridge.
Like I'd been walking,
running, tripping, dancing
on this fragile, rocky edge.
This wicked edge where I was
always trying to keep from falling.
And on one side was who I used to be
and on the other was who I was trying to be.

Only now I had fallen hard. Lost my balance and fallen
from a misstep so bad, I didn't know if the damage was fixable.

AND THEN A THOUGHT

came into my head.

A thought that was easier,

felt better to believe.

A thought whispering that

I had been *pushed* over the edge.

I had been dared to walk along it.

Someone had wanted

to see me fall. Someone

who never thought

I was brave enough to even try.

I KNEW KING WOULD COME THAT NIGHT

My mother
took my phone.

I didn't protest,
handed it over.

Then I just waited.
Soon I saw the light

behind the curtain.
When I got in the truck,

he put it in gear like usual.
As if nothing had changed.

SO

King said. I waited.
You're in it pretty deep, huh?

I stared out the window.
Yeah, I'm in it
pretty deep.

I knew you would be.
That was pretty messed up.
Funny pic though.

I felt sick inside.
It wasn't funny.

WELL, SHE DIDN'T THINK SO

He chewed
his gum slowly.

Who? I asked,
thinking about Taylor.

What would she say
when she saw me?

Principal, he answered.
I didn't understand.

*You talked to the principal?
About this? Today?*

*Yeah, well she called me
in there. For once I wasn't
the one in trouble.*

I IMAGINED HIM SMILING

going into the office,
innocent this time.

Why did she want to talk to you?
I asked him.

People like to blame
crap on me. She was

trying to get me for this.
I guess people didn't
know where it started.

They figured it came from me.
But it didn't.

I CONNECTED THE DOTS

King, did you tell her it was me?

It was, he said.

My brain felt like
it was exploding.
He had sold me out.
He said,

Look, I wasn't going to go down for this.
I mean, I screw up, but not like that.

There were no words in my brain.

He's a special kid, Helen.
Jeez, that's...bad.

He was right. I knew that.
But all I could think at the time
was that he betrayed me.

Had he ever cared
about me at all?

Don't act like this isn't
the kind of girl you wanted,
I shot back at him.

His neck pulled back.
What?

I CHANGED FOR YOU

I became this
person for you,
I said.

Uh. He shook his head.
If you "changed," you did that for you.
Don't put your crap on me.

But I did put it on him,
wanting it to be his fault.

I wanted to be able to tell myself
that I wasn't a bad person. Just
let myself get carried away.

Pushed over the edge
by someone

who thought it would be fun
to see me fall. I told him
I hated him.

He fought back at me,
parked outside his house now.

YOU HATE ME?

He said.

Why? Because poor you
got in some real trouble?
I guess white kids
ain't used to that.
Usually they just pin it
on someone else, right?
You get a slap on the wrist
and get to go home.
That's called privilege.
Well, it don't work like that here.
Why should you get to walk away fine?
It ain't so fun playing
the bad girl with the Indian boyfriend
when you can't blame him
for your crap, huh?

I was stunned.
He had never called me out
for my skin color before.
I had never thought of it
like an advantage
in that way.

WE CALLED EACH OTHER NAMES

Yelling now.
He got out

and slapped his palm
on my window,

telling me to get out while I
screamed back at him.

He pushed his key into the lock
and ripped open my door,

then grabbed my arm hard
and pulled. I fell out

onto the ground
and he yelled, *Get up!*

Fear was pumping
through me now,

and I looked for a place to run,
my arm throbbing where he held it.

Out of nowhere, someone
ran up between us.

KORA'S GRIP WAS STRONG

She held my arm and King's
and tore them apart.

Both of us blanked.
We let her push us away.
Get in the car!

she yelled at me. She pointed
to a small, green Camry

parked in the street, still running.
I didn't protest. I stomped away.
She turned to her brother.

From the Camry I watched
them yelling for a while.

Then I was startled to see them hug.
They latched onto each other and
I heard King crying. Big deep sobs.

Then they walked
together into the house.

A HALF HOUR LATER

Kora took me home.
We were both calmer.

She said the neighbors
had called her. Didn't want to
get the cops without giving her

a chance to stop things.

We sat in the strangeness,
feeling our history in the car.

I didn't want this to happen,
she said, while we made our way
back to Damon's trailer.

Her jawbone got tight.
King's always had a temper.
After my grandma died…

She trailed off for a moment.
Things got pretty bad.
The road flew by beneath us.

I remembered being warned
about Kora's temper.

WHY DID YOU ATTACK ME?

I asked, because even though
it felt like our problem was over,
I was still mad at her.

I was still trying to understand
all the things that had gone wrong.

I thought I could scare you,
that day in the gym. I saw

the look he gave you from the office
and I knew he would go after you.

His head…it isn't in a good place.
For the first time, she
looked like she might cry.

Then I realized she hadn't been
attacking me.
In her own way,
she'd been protecting me.

I SWALLOWED HARD

He was really close
with your grandma, wasn't he? I asked.

She nodded her head.
It's not that King
wanted to hurt you,

she told me. *I didn't either.*
I cocked an eyebrow.

Sorry, she said. *I just*
wanted you to stay away.
I knew King was looking

for someone to…
I cut in.

Play with?

Her mouth turned down.
He was looking for someone new.

I WAS LOOKING FOR SOMEONE, TOO

I admitted. And I finally
knew that to be true.
Someone. Anyone.

At first it had been Taylor,
and then it was King.

I had been hurt
when I found out King
didn't really care about me.

But the truth was that I didn't think
I had ever cared about him either.

It was the standing he gave me,
the way he made people look at me,
like I belonged where he was.

Neither of us had been fair, and
he was right. I made the choice to be cruel.

Kora gave a short nod,
then pulled into Damon's driveway.
Thanks, I said.

She didn't say anything.
I got out and walked into the house.

Part Six

TAYLOR AND HARRY LEFT SMOHOLLA

And so did I, expelled.
I wrote them a long

apology letter,
but I never heard back

from Taylor
or her family.

I knew
I deserved that.

MOM SAID

that she heard they moved
somewhere near Yakima.

They had family over there,
didn't have to deal

with the unwanted attention
I put on them here.

They left their home
because of you,

she told me.
Don't ever forget that.

Guilt sits in me,
a rock heavy on my gut,

and I know that
I never can.

WHEN I KNEW HOW, I APOLOGIZED

to my mother.
I told her

about being bullied,
about feeling so alone.

She said she was sorry
for pushing me too hard.

Told me we couldn't
change the past.

We could only make
better choices for the future.

Such a teacher thing to say.
But of course she was right.

DAMON ALSO HAD ADVICE

He came to my room one night,
knocked softly on the door.

He sat in my desk chair
and leaned forward,

elbows over knees,
but didn't say anything

for a long time.
I sat on my bed, waiting.

He looked up at me.
People won't forget what you did.

I looked down, tears pooling.
I picked at my blanket.

I was ready
for him to yell at me.

BUT HIS VOICE STAYED LOW

You need to show
you're better than that now.

I nodded my head.
In the fall I would start

at Omak High School,
somewhere to try again.

Damon knew I was nervous.
There were a lot of people there

who knew and loved Harry.
And there were lots of posts online

from people around town. People who thought
I should have been punished much worse.

I KNOW IT'S BEEN TOUGH

he said. *But things are tough for everybody.*
If people use what's happened to them

as an excuse to act like jerks,
they'll never heal. Or grow.

You saw what happened
when you let fear push you around.

He stood up to leave.

You know better now, he said.
Make the choice to be brave this time.

I wondered, could I be brave?
Brave enough to be

the person I say that I am
instead of letting other people decide?

Before he reached the door,
I made a choice.

Damon? I asked.
Can you help me?

I STARTED TO LEARN

In the next few weeks,
Damon answered

every question I had about
Native culture and tradition.

He took me to ceremonies
and powwows, showed me

dances and songs
that opened my eyes.

I realized that mostly,
people wanted to share

their customs. They were kind
and giving. So proud to show

their families and their hard work.
I had been ignorant. I saw that now.

The problem wasn't just that I didn't know.
The problem was I didn't want to know.

I realized that when I had been afraid,
I had only needed to ask for help.

THE NIGHT BEFORE SCHOOL STARTS AGAIN

Mom and I sit with Damon on the porch.
He burns sage in a well-used abalone shell.

The smoke lifts away
toward the heavy sun hanging low.

I am wrapped in an old quilt
and Mom reads a book,

bouncing her slippered foot.
Damon looks for deer

in the surrounding fields.
Coyotes start to howl

from beyond the brush.
Damon tells me a story.

It's about Coyote.
The Creator sent Coyote to earth

to finish the people,
Damon says. He looks at me.

People don't know
they aren't finished yet.

I turn to the fading summer sun
and breathe deeply, willing the sage

to take out the bad and leave some good.

AFTER MOM AND DAMON ARE IN BED

I walk around my room,
setting out jeans

and the T-shirt I will wear tomorrow.
I hear a noise outside.

I glance at my window,
the way I have a million times

since the night King and I fought.
The corner of the curtain hangs limp.

Not folded back anymore.
But sometimes I go over to it,

looking for his truck.
Even though I know he's not coming.

I DON'T TALK TO THE BIGELKS ANYMORE

Sometimes I see King
in town. Playing basketball

in the park or out to eat
with his friends.

We don't say anything,
don't even make eye contact.

Really there's nothing
to say. Nothing left

to get from
each other.

I THINK ABOUT HIM AS I FALL ASLEEP

And I remember
the monsters in both of us.

How I ignored
a boy who needed help

for a King who helped me.
I see him now.

We're both
back up on that edge,

both holding on to
any balance we can find,

trying not to fall.

WANT TO KEEP READING?

If you liked this book, check out another book from West 44 Books:

MORE THAN ANGER
BY LEXI BRUCE

ISBN: 9781538382639

FAMILY TIME

Anna, get off your phone,
Mom says,
It's time for dinner.
Dad's home. We're going out.

I sigh, text Jess, my best friend,
that we'll talk later.

I want to hear all about her new
boyfriend, Sam.
But for now it's family time.
Strictly enforced—
three dinners a week.

Even if it's only
a chance for them
to show the world
what a mess
we are as a family.

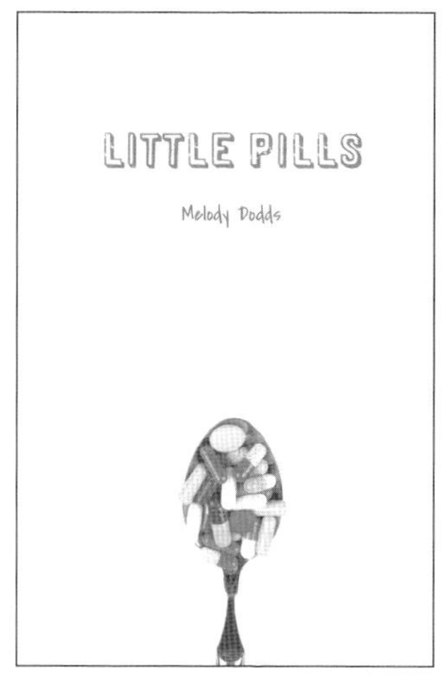

Check out more books at:
www.west44books.com

An imprint of Enslow Publishing
WEST 44 BOOKS™

ABOUT THE AUTHOR

Nicole Elizabeth grew up in Central New York and attended Canisius College, where she received a degree in English and creative writing. She served as an AmeriCorps volunteer through Jesuit Volunteer Corps Northwest at Paschal-Sherman Indian School in Omak, Washington, on the Colville Indian Reservation. There she fostered significant relationships with the kids, community members, and fellow volunteers while teaching and tutoring in reading.